Look Out! Look Out! Tractor About!

JOAN DALGLEISH

Illustrated by Pete Joison and Gordon Clarke

sundance

The Story Characters

Sid Bacon
An old farmer.

Jenny
Sid's trusty horse.

Ken Bacon
Sid's son.

Keith Brown
The farmer
next door.

The Story Setting

TABLE OF CONTENTS

Chapter 4
The Tractor

CHAPTER 1

Sid Needs a Tractor

Sid Bacon and his horse, Jenny, had worked as a team for years.

They were friends.

7

Jenny pulled the plow that dug the soil. She walked along slowly while Sid spread the seed.

Sid's son, Ken, milked the cows. He fixed the fences. He took the crops to market in an old truck.

"Why don't you get a tractor, Dad?"
Ken asked. "Keith Brown has one."

"No," said his father. "Good old
Jenny is good enough for me."

One day a man from the city came to the farm. He laughed at Jenny pulling the plow.

The man showed Sid a photo of a brand new tractor.

"Horses are too slow," the man said. "A tractor will do the work in half of the time."

"Come on, Dad," said Ken. "Our fences are down. Our cattle are straying. You could use the extra time to help me. Why don't you buy a tractor?"

"I'll think about it," said his father.

"I'd have more time," Sid told Jenny. "We could go for rides together. That is much better than walking up and down the same field all day, eh?"

Jenny blew in his ear.

CHAPTER 2

Sid Buys a Tractor

The tractor came on the back of a large truck.

"It's easier to drive than a horse—
no feed to mix, no coat to brush.
Just fill her with fuel and away
she goes," said the driver.

Jenny watched as Sid drove off on the new tractor.

The tractor was noisy. Sid had
to wear earplugs. The dogs barked
at the tractor. Birds flew out of
the trees.

Jenny neighed loudly and trotted
away in disgust.

The tractor plowed the field in half the usual time.

"Wonderful!" Sid cried. "That was the best money I ever spent."

By noon Sid had plowed a second field. The sun was high in the sky.

"Lunch time!" Sid said, and he jumped off the tractor. He forgot about the brake. He forgot to turn the engine off.

"Whoa," Sid said as he walked away.

CHAPTER 3

Trail of Disaster

Chug. Chug. Chug. The tractor moved off by itself. It went across the field and into the next one.

The tractor ran over a crop of young corn plants. It squashed them flat.

Chug. Chug. Chug. The tractor kept going. It went through a fence and onto the road.

Some sheep were eating grass on the side of the road. The noise of the tractor made the sheep run.

The tractor chased them down the road and into the farm next door.

The tractor kept on going.

Keith Brown was taking some pumpkins to the market. The pumpkins were piled high on the truck.

He drove around a corner.

"Aahh!" he yelled. "Look out! Look out! Tractor about!"

Keith Brown swung the steering
wheel. The truck tipped over.

Hundreds of pumpkins bounced and rolled over the road.

He stopped the truck. He was very angry.

"Look what you've done!" he cried.

He picked up a pumpkin. He threw it at the tractor. He shook his fist in the air. "Come back here!"

Chug. Chug. Chug. The tractor kept on going. It bumped over a cattle grid and back into Sid's yard.

The hens were scratching in the dust.
"Brark! Brark! Skwark! Skwark!"

They flew up in the air. They flew
sideways. They flew all ways. The
hens flapped and cackled as the
tractor scared them all over the
place.

The tractor kept going.

CHAPTER 4

The Tractor Comes Back

Sid Bacon's wife, Liz, was hanging out the wash.

"Aaah! Eeeek!"

The tractor ran into the clothesline.

"Stop! Stop!" she cried.

The tractor kept going, taking the clothesline with it.

Clothes flew from either side. Shirts
and jeans flapped in the wind.

"It's heading for the pond!" cried Liz. She began to run. "Look out! Look out! Tractor about!"

Sid had finished his lunch. He walked outside and stretched his arms into the air.

When Sid opened his eyes, he saw
his new tractor racing down a bank
toward the pond.

"Oh no!" he yelled. "Who let my tractor loose?"

He began to run.

"Whoa! Whoa!" he cried.
"Whooaa!!"

Chug. Chug. Chug. The tractor kept on going.

Ken was bending over to fix the
water pump.

The tractor came closer, and closer, and closer.

Ken was testing the water pump.

Bump!

Splash! Ken went head first into the pond.

Sid jumped up on the tractor. At the very edge of the pond, Sid made it stop.

Ken came up out of the water. He laughed. "I almost got plowed. I'm glad you didn't dig me up."

Sid looked back over the path of the runaway tractor. He saw the broken clothesline, the cackling hens, and the smashed pumpkins. He could see scattered sheep and flat corn stalks.

"What a stupid tractor!" Sid said.

Ken and Liz looked at each other but did not say a word.

Then Sid remembered. He was the one who had forgotten to turn off the engine. "Oh," he said. His face went red.

That night, Sid locked the tractor in the shed. He took some carrots to his horse.

"Sorry I'm late, Jenny," Sid said, patting her mane. "I had to clean up the mess."

Jenny snorted into his hand as she ate the carrots.

"Well, old girl," said Sid. "A tractor can do the work in half the time. But it's double the trouble, by golly!"

GLOSSARY

cackled
made a sharp noise

cattle grid
metal strips
to stop cattle

disgust
strong dislike

fuel
gas used to run
trucks and tractors

plow
a machine used
to dig up ground

runaway
moving
without a driver

scattered
moved in
all directions

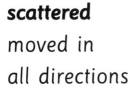

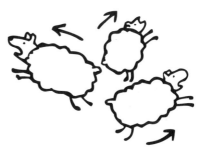

snorted
made a noise
like a pig

Joan Dalgleish

Joan has had ten books published for children including *Albert's Birthday* and *Dog on a Diet*. She loves visiting schools to talk about books and reading. She is a writer, actor, and passionate walker.

Pete Joison and Gordon Clarke

These two run a graphic design studio. It's called Uddi Uddi, and they create graphics that entertain. They each have a wife and one baby girl. Pete's favorite color is cheesecake yellow, and Gordon's favorite number is pi. Life is good!

sundance
A Haights Cross Communications Company

Published by Sundance Publishing
P.O. Box 740, One Beeman Road, Northborough, MA 01532

Copyright © text Joan Dalgleish
Copyright © illustrations Pete Joison and Gordon Clarke

First published 1999 as Sparklers by
Blake Education, Locked Bag 2022, Glebe 2037, Australia
Exclusive United States Distribution: Sundance Publishing

ISBN 0-7608-4939-0